STORMY WEATHER

SIMON SPOTLIGHT
An imprint of Simon & Schuster Children's Publishing Division
1230 Avenue of the Americas
New York, New York 10020

Based on the TV series Rugrats® created by
Klasky/Csupo Inc. and Paul Germain as seen on Nickelodeon®

First Simon Spotlight Edition, 1997

Manufactured in the United States of America

15 14 13 12 11 10

Library of Congress Cataloging-in-Publication Data
Wigand, Molly.
Stormy weather / by Molly Wigand; pictures by Barry Goldberg — 1st U.S. ed.
p. cm. — (Ready-to-Read.)
Summary: A group of babies comfort each other as a storm rages outside.
ISBN 0-689-81259-0
[1. Babies—Fiction. 2. Storms—Fiction.]
I. Goldberg, Barry, 1960- ill. II. Title. III. Series.
PZ7.W6375St   1997
96-24132
[E]—dc20
CIP   AC

STORMY WEATHER

by Molly Wigand
illustrated by Barry Goldberg

Ready-to-Read

Simon Spotlight/Nickelodeon

"Look, kids!" said Tommy's mom.
"'Dummy Bears' is on. You can watch TV
while I fix dinner."

Angelica made a face. "Stupid baby
show! When I'm grown-up—"

"Beep! Beep! Beep!" A loud noise came
from the TV. "We now bring you a special
weather report," a man said.

"Heavy storms will move through this area," said the TV man. He pointed to a big map.

"Look! Some baby drew on his map!" said Angelica. "Bet he was mad!"

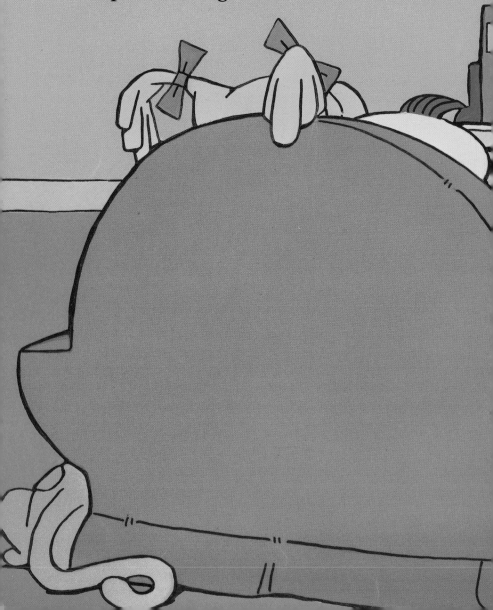

The weatherman kept talking. "Be ready to take cover. We might even see a tornado or two."

"A tomato? Who cares?" said Chuckie. "We see tomatoes every day!"

Angelica's eyes got big. "You stupid baby," she said. "He means giant tomatoes that spin. Bazillions of them fall from the sky. They go right through your umbrella! You can get soaked with tomato juice!"

"Yuck!" said Phil and Lil. "We hate tomato juice!"

Tommy thought for a minute. "At least it's not giant spinning spinach!"

The man on TV was still talking. "Now let's check the radar screen," he said.

"Radar?" said Chuckie. "Isn't that Reptar's cousin?"

"Yeah!" said Tommy.

The weatherman sounded scared. "There's a cold front coming this way," he said.

"I had a cold front once,"
Chuckie said. "I spilled juice all over
my tummy." The babies laughed.

The weatherman kept talking.
"When that cold front meets a warm
front . . . watch out! The winds could blow
down power lines."

Thunder growled softly.
"W-w-w-what is that?" asked Chuckie.
Spike jumped up in his lap.

"It's the power lions! They're mad
'cause they got blowed over!" said
Angelica.

17

Tommy shook his head. "It's not power lions! It's a marching band getting ready for a parade."

Spike's tail wagged a little.

"We like parades!" said Phil and Lil.
The babies marched around the
room and said, "Toot, toot!" They
weren't scared any more. Until . . .

Lightning flashed. Then loud thunder crashed!

Angelica started to cry. "Okay, Tommy Smarty-pants. If this is a parade, what was that big bang?"

Spike ran under the couch.

"The light was a camera taking a picture of our marching band," said Tommy. "And the noise was all the people clapping for us."

All of the sudden, the sky was really dark.

Chuckie said, "I'm scared."

"Don't worry," Tommy said. He patted Chuckie's hand. "You know how Mom makes our room dark for nap time? Now it's nap time for the birdies. That's why their mommies made the sky so dark."

Suddenly the storm pounded the house. "Oh dear," said Tommy's mom. "It's raining cats and dogs." She ran to close the windows.

Spike peeked out from under the couch. He ran to the window. Then he howled sadly.

"Mom is mixed up," said Tommy. "It's raining plain old water!"

The babies covered their ears. They covered their eyes. They waited and waited for the storm to end.

And after awhile, it did. The rain stopped. The thunder stopped. And the sun started to shine.

Tommy's mom opened the front door. "You kids can go outside," she said. "Maybe there's a rainbow."

Angelica laughed out loud. "That's silly," she said. "Everybody knows rainbows aren't real!"

The babies all ran out the door.
Chuckie pointed up in the sky. "Look!
It's red and yellow and purple and

green . . . just like in pictures! See,
Angelica? It's a real live rainbow."

"Wow!" said Tommy.

"Rainbows are the best part of a rainy day!" said Chuckie.

"Oh no, they're not!" said Tommy.

"What's the best part?" asked Phil and Lil.

"What could be better than rainbows?" asked Angelica.

"Puddles!" yelled Tommy.
And the babies just had to agree.